D0382463

© HEMMAHOS
Let's go, says the Pencil
Project manager: Lena Allblom, IKEA of Sweden AB
Project coordinator: Anders Truedsson, TITEL Books AB
Text: Ulf Stark
Illustrations: Malin Unnborn
Typesetting: Gyllene Snittet AB, Sweden
Translation: Comactiva Language Partner AB, Sweden
Produced by IKEA of Sweden AB
Paper: Arcoset FSC
Printing: Litopat S.p.A., Italy 2016
TITEL Books AB for IKEA of Sweden AB. All rights reserved.

We aim to provide as much inspiration as possible, but with minimal impact on the
environment. All our books take the environment into account in every stage of production,
from the choice of paper to how we distribute our printed material.

The book you are holding is printed on paper that meets all the requirements for responsible
forestry. This means, for example, that the paper raw material comes from trees that are
certified to originate from a sustainably managed forest. We print using vegetable-based
printing inks without solvents, and the printers are located close to our large markets to
avoid long-distance transport to you.

We are also working to develop the printed medium so that it minimises impact on the
environment in the future. Read more about our environmental work at www.ikea.co.uk

LET'S GO, SAYS THE PENCIL

Ulf Stark

Malin Unnborn

In the red house with the stripy roof live three friends: The Alarm Clock, the Cactus and the Toothbrush. They have lived there for as long as they can remember.

Because they have no legs or feet, they have never been out of the house.

But that's okay.

They like it where they are.

"What would we do out there?" asks the Toothbrush. "There's so much noise that my hair would stand on end."

"And who would I wake in the morning?" ticks the Alarm Clock.

"And whose teeth would I brush?" adds the Toothbrush.

They are both very proud that they are so USEFUL.

As they talk, the Cactus feels sad.

"But what use am I?" she sighs. "I'm just a useless little plant that you could prick yourself on."

"But you're green and beautiful," says the Alarm Clock.

"Not really," says the Cactus.

"Well, we think so. And we love you as well," says the Toothbrush.

And then they don't say much more. They don't need to.

But when the Alarm Clock looks at the Toothbrush, her heart beats stronger:

"Tick tock, tick tock." And when the Toothbrush looks at her, he thinks, "Oh, she's so lovely and red."

And so the days pass, one after the other.

But one night, the Pencil comes to the house. No one knows how. They don't even know what he *is*. Suddenly he's just there in the doorway, with his pink eraser foot, looking terribly important. Tall and yellow, with a head that finishes up in a sharp point.

"Who are you?" hisses the Cactus, who is not sure she likes having visitors.

"I am the Pencil," says the stranger. "Haven't you heard of me?"

"No we haven't," says the Toothbrush.

"I thought EVERYONE had," says the Pencil. "I'm famous. I draw and I write, fairy tales and all sorts of things."

"What do you mean, draw?" asks the Alarm Clock.

"Like this," says the Pencil.

There is a piece of paper sticking out of a drawer. The Pencil pulls it out and puts it on the floor. He bends over and moves his head against the paper to make black lines.

"See?" he says when he has finished. "See what I can draw?"

"No," says the Cactus.

"But, oh gosh… that's *me*!" says the Alarm Clock, and turns even redder than before. "With numbers and hands and everything."

"Yes well, that's only black and white," snorts the Toothbrush.

"Well, I think it's a lovely picture," says the Alarm Clock, smiling as much as a clock can smile.

"But who would want to draw me?" says the Cactus gloomily. "I'm just a round ball with prickles all over me."

"I would," says the Pencil.

And so he draws her too, so nicely that she is almost happy.

But the Toothbrush doesn't want to be a picture.

"Oh no," he snorts so the toothpaste goes everywhere.

That night, the Pencil draws all kinds of things.

He fills the paper with things the others have never seen before. Things that can fly in the sky. Things that go vroom and run on wheels. And things that grow out of the ground and are called trees.

"Does anybody know what this is?" he asks.

"No, what is it?" says the Cactus.

"A house," says the Pencil. "Like the one you live in. Did you not even know that? You don't seem to know much about the world."

"No," says the Alarm Clock. "We've never been outside the door. How come you know so much?"

"Oh, I've seen and done all sorts of things," he says. "You can't imagine how much there is to see if you were only brave enough to leave the house."

"Please tell us!" begs the Alarm Clock.

"Oh please leave him alone," says the Toothbrush. "I'm sure he is tired after spinning his head round on a piece of paper like that."

But the Pencil tells them about all his adventures – he makes most of them up – until he can't manage any more. Then he takes a bow and writes:

GOOD NIGHT

The Toothbrush and Cactus fall asleep almost immediately. The Pencil takes a while. But the Alarm Clock is awake for a long time.

She sees the Pencil lying there, all straight and yellow, and thinks: "What a hero!"

And she looks at the houses through the window and thinks: "How wonderful it would be to see THE WORLD. But how could that possibly ever happen when I have no feet?"

10

GOOD NIGHT

The next morning, the Alarm Clock rings early. She can wait no longer.

"Imagine if you could show us the world," she says to the Pencil. "You have made me want to see it so-o-o much!"

"But isn't it ever so dangerous out there?" asks the Cactus.

"Yes, it's probably not suitable for you," snorts the Pencil – he has made a lot of stories up and is worried the others will find out. "After all, not everyone is as brave as me."

"Nonsense," says the Toothbrush. "I am! In fact I reckon I'm even braver. Unfortunately though, we don't have any feet to walk with."

"I can soon sort that out," says the Pencil.

And he draws legs and feet on all of them. And also small arms and hands so they can carry their bags.

But he has to do without, because he can't draw on himself.

"There you go," he says. "You are ready now."

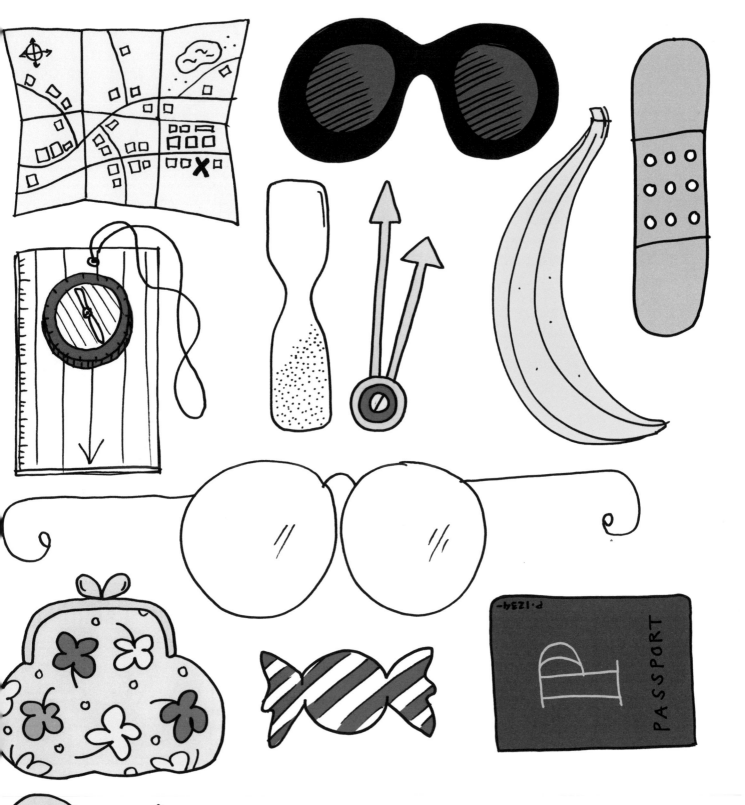

"We just have to pack first," says the Alarm Clock.

She stuffs a duvet cover into her bag. She is going to lie on it and do some sunbathing. After all, the Pencil said the sun is always shining out there. The Cactus takes a pillow to rest on in case she gets tired.

"Let's go," says the Pencil.

Outside, the sun is shining. There are white clouds blowing across the sky. The three friends are enjoying trying out their new legs.

"Whoa!" says the Toothbrush, wobbling around.

He finds it hard to balance because he's so tall. And he's also carrying two bags.

The Cactus smells the flowers and plants they pass.

"These are my relatives," she says. "They are beautiful and smell nice. That's more than anyone can say about me. I'm not good for anything."

The Alarm Clock does a little dance, she is so happy.

And out in front is the Pencil, hopping along on his eraser foot and pointing out all kinds of things with his pointy head.

"That's a bird," he says, nodding towards an aeroplane.

"You're so clever!" says the Alarm Clock, full of admiration.

"Is it time for a rest soon?" puffs the Toothbrush.

They have seen big houses in the city.

And small houses in the country.

"So where are all these dangers and adventures someone was boasting about?" snorts the Toothbrush. "We may as well go home now."

"I must rest my legs a bit," puffs the Cactus.

"And I would like to sunbathe a little more," says the Alarm Clock.

But just then, a big black cloud blows over the sky and blocks the sun out.

And before they know it, the wind blows and it starts raining.

It pours down and soaks them all through. The water is rushing along in the gutters.

"Well?" shouts the Pencil. "How about this for an adventure!"

And it certainly is. Suddenly a gust of wind blows the Pencil right over. He spins round and round, and falls into the gutter.

"Help! Help!" he cries.

And off he floats on the stream of rainwater.

The Alarm Clock rings with alarm because she can see where the Pencil is going. Straight towards a drain hole!

Without hesitating, the Toothbrush grabs the Cactus and dives in after the Pencil. He swims as fast as he can, holding the Cactus in front of him.

"What are you doing?" says the Cactus, spitting out water.

"You must stick one of your prickles in his foot," gasps the Toothbrush. "It's his only chance!"

But they're not going to make it.

And that's when the Alarm Clock does it.

She concentrates all her thoughts on the Pencil. She holds her breath, and her ticking heart stops inside her. She makes time stand still for the Pencil, just as he is about to be washed down the drain hole. Just in time, the Cactus manages to stick a prickle into the Pencil's foot.

24

Together, they manage to get the Pencil up onto the pavement.

"Thank you for saving my life," says the Pencil.

He doesn't sound so tough now.

"Gosh, you're ever so brave," says the Alarm Clock to the Toothbrush.

And the Toothbrush smiles for the first time that day. And the Cactus smiles too, because now she knows what she is good at.

"I am good at stopping Pencils from going down drain holes!" she says. "Sometimes it's not so bad being prickly."

After all their adventures, they need to rest. The Alarm Clock is absolutely exhausted, because there is nothing so strenuous as stopping time.

A little way off they see an empty caravan. They go inside. The Alarm Clock spreads her duvet cover out on the floor. The Cactus sits on her pillow. And the Pencil lays down and holds his eraser foot up towards her.

"Blow it better please," he says. "I'm so grateful to you for saving my life. But your prickle pricked my foot."

The Cactus blows it better until it has stopped raining.

"Gosh, I'm getting late!" says the Alarm Clock.

"Yes, time to go home and brush some teeth," says the Toothbrush.

And off the four friends go.

The Alarm Clock next to the Toothbrush. And the Pencil next to the Cactus, because – as he puts it – he has become rather attached to her.

"I'm not going to make so much stuff up in future," he says ruefully. "It only leads to trouble."

"Oh yes you are," says the Cactus. "You can tell us bedtime stories every evening."

And when they get home, that's exactly what he does.
A really exciting story, just like this one.